Up

I Like to Read® books, created by award-winning picture book artists as well as talented newcomers, instill confidence and the joy of reading in new readers.

We want to hear every new reader say, "I like to read!"

_____

Visit our website for flash cards, activities, and more about the series:
www.holidayhouse.com/I-Like-to-Read/
#ILTR
This book has been tested by an educational expert and determined to be a guided reading level B.

Up

Joe Cepeda

I Like to Read®

HOLIDAY HOUSE • NEW YORK

I LIKE TO READ is a registered trademark of Holiday House, Inc.

Copyright © 2016 by Joe Cepeda
All Rights Reserved
HOLIDAY HOUSE is registered in the U.S. Patent and Trademark Office.
Printed and bound in April 2017 at Hong Kong Graphics and Printing Ltd., China.
The artwork was created with digital tools.
www.holidayhouse.com
3 5 7 9 10 8 6 4 2

Library of Congress Cataloging-in-Publication Data

Names: Cepeda, Joe, author, illustrator.
Title: Up / Joe Cepeda.
Description: First edition. | New York : Holiday House, [2016] | Series: I
like to read | Summary: "On a very windy day, a boy stands by a window
with his pinwheel and is suddenly whisked into the sky where he can see a
pig, a hen, a cow, and a sheep"— Provided by publisher.
Identifiers: LCCN 2015045420 | ISBN 9780823436552 (hardcover)
Subjects: | CYAC: Winds—Fiction. | Domestic animals—Fiction.
Classification: LCC PZ7.C3184 Up 2016 | DDC [E]—dc23 LC record available at http://lccn.loc.gov/2015045420
ISBN 978-0-8234-3887-7 (paperback)

For the Licanos

Look.

Look.

I go up.

I see a hen.

I see a sheep.

I see a cow.

I see a pig.

They go home.

I go home.

I Like to Read®

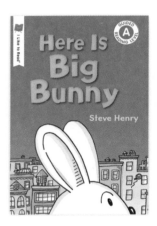

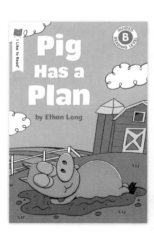

Visit http://www.holidayhouse.com/I-Like-to-Read/ for more about I Like to Read®
books, including flash cards, reproducibles, and the complete list of titles.